The ANNE of GREEN GABLES TREASURY of DAYS

CAROLYN STROM COLLINS

CHRISTINA WYSS ERIKSSON

VIKING

VIKING

Published by the Penguin Group

Penguin Books Canada Ltd, 10 Alcorn Avenue, Toronto, Ontario, Canada M4V 3B2

Penguin Books Ltd, 27 Wrights Lane, London W8 5TZ, England

Viking Penguin, a division of Penguin Books USA Inc., 375 Hudson Street, New York, New York 10014, U.S.A.

Penguin Books Australia Ltd, Ringwood, Victoria, Australia

Penguin Books (NZ) Ltd, 182–190 Wairau Road, Auckland 10, New Zealand

Penguin Books Ltd, Registered Offices: Harmondsworth, Middlesex, England

First published 1994

1 3 5 7 9 10 8 6 4 2

Design by Pronk&Associates

Printed and bound in Italy on acid neutral paper

Canadian Cataloguing in Publication Data

Collins, Carolyn.
   The Anne of Green Gables treasury of days
ISBN 0-670-85508-1

1. Montgomery, L. M. (Lucy Maud), 1874–1942 — Calendars.
2. Perpetual calendars.   I. Eriksson, Christina Wyss.   II. Title.
PS8526.068A75   1994   C813'.52   C93–094940-4
PR9199.2.M66A75   1994

American Library of Congress Cataloguing in Publication Data Available

INTRODUCTION

The Anne of Green Gables Treasury of Days is a collection of especially beautiful nature quotations from the eight books that make up the Anne series, created by L. M. Montgomery — *Anne of Green Gables, Anne of Avonlea, Anne of the Island, Anne of Windy Poplars, Anne's House of Dreams, Anne of Ingleside, Rainbow Valley,* and *Rilla of Ingleside* — as well as notations on some of the other authors quoted throughout the Anne books.

One of L. M. Montgomery's gifts was her ability to describe the natural beauty of the settings in which her stories took place, usually on Prince Edward Island. Every season of the year, every whim of weather, every sunrise or sunset evoked in Montgomery a deep spiritual response that she articulated with great sensitivity. We have compiled some of her richest and most descriptive passages to correspond to the month or season in which they are found in the Anne books so that readers can enjoy them, a day at a time, throughout each and every year.

We include also, on the birthdays of their authors, quotations from Montgomery's own favourite writings which she cited often in her work.

There is space provided with each date for the reader to make her own notes, perhaps the birthday of a friend, an important event in her own life or an observation of a particularly lovely, special moment.

We hope that this *Treasury of Days* gives readers a greater sense of the exceptional beauty of Anne's world and, most importantly, that they will recognize it in their own.

"The year is a book, isn't it, Marilla? Spring's pages are written in Mayflowers and violets, summer's in roses, autumn's in red maple leaves, and winter in holly and evergreen."

JANUARY

Anne came dancing home in the purple
winter twilight across the snowy places.
Afar in the southwest was the great
shimmering pearl-like sparkle of an
evening star that was pale golden and
ethereal rose over gleaming white
spaces and dark glens of spruce.

JANUARY

1 **New Year's Day**
"Welcome, New Year," said Captain Jim,
bowing as the last stroke died away. "I wish you
all the best year of your lives, mates."

2 The night was clear and frosty, all ebony of
shadow and silver of snowy slope ...

3 ... big stars were shining over the silent fields ...

4 ... here and there the dark pointed firs stood
up with snow powdering their branches and the
wind whistling through them.

5 Anne had gone home in the wonderful, white-
frosted winter morning ...

6   … they crossed the long white field and walked
under the glittering fairy arch of the Lovers' Lane
maples.

7   "I'm so glad I live in a world where there are
white frosts, aren't you?"

8   The tinkles of sleigh bells among the snowy hills
came like elfin chimes through the frosty air, but
their music was not sweeter than the song in
Anne's heart and on her lips.

9   The winter weeks slipped by.

10   It was an unusually mild winter, with so little snow that Anne and Diana could go to school nearly every day by way of the Birch Path.

11   … the winter passed away in a round of pleasant duties and studies.

JANUARY

12 The kitchen was deserted and she sat down by the window in the fast falling wintry twilight.

13 A pale chilly moon looked out behind a bank of purple clouds in the west.

14 The sky faded out, but the strip of yellow along the western horizon grew brighter and fiercer, as if all the stray gleams of light were concentrating in one spot …

15 … the distant hills, rimmed with priest-like firs, stood out in dark distinctness against it.

16 "January so far has been a month of cold grey days, with an occasional storm whirling across the harbour and filling Spook's Lane with drifts."

17 "… last night we had a silver thaw and today the sun shone."

18 "My maple grove was a place of unimaginable splendours. Even the commonplaces had been made lovely."

19 "Every bit of wire fencing was a wonder of crystal lace."

20 Big, white drifts heaped themselves about the little house, and palms of frost covered its windows.

21 The harbour ice grew harder and thicker, until the Four Winds people began their usual winter travelling over it.

---

22 George Gordon, Lord Byron, was born on this
date in 1788. Anne referred to his epic poem
"Childe Harold's Pilgrimage" as she left Prince
Edward Island for "Redmond College"
in Nova Scotia.

---

23 The gulf froze over, and the Four Winds light
flashed no more.

---

24 Anne and Leslie took long snowshoe tramps
together ... over the fields, or across the harbour
after storms, or through the woods beyond
the Glen.

25 Robert Burns, beloved poet of Scotland, was born in 1759. Captain Jim welcomed Anne and Leslie Moore to the Four Winds Point Lighthouse with Burns' famous quote, "We'll 'take a cup o' kindness yet for auld lang syne'" the evening they delivered his "life book" to him.

26 It was … a streaky winter … all thaws and freezes that kept Ingleside decorated with fantastic fringes of icicles.

27 Charles Dodson ("Lewis Carroll"), creator of *Alice in Wonderland*, was born on this date in 1832. Anne often referred to "shoes and ships and sealing wax/And cabbages and kings" from his poem "The Walrus and the Carpenter."

28 There were rabbit trails in the snow to follow and great crusted fields over which you raced with your shadows and glistening hills for coasting and new skates to be tried out on the pond in the chill, rosy world of winter sunset.

29 Poet Sarah Chauncey Woolsey was born on this date in 1835. On the morning after Anne's "Jonah Day," a fresh snowfall prompted her to sing these lines from Woolsey's poem 'Susan Coolidge":

"Every morn is a fresh beginning,
Every morn is the world made new."

30 ... the twilight crept softly down over the white valley and the evening star shone over the grey maple grove.

31 Anne sat up o' nights to pore over seed catalogues in January and February.

FEBRUARY

"Diana's birthday is in February and
mine is in March."

1 There was a magnificent sunset, and the snowy
hills and deep blue water of the St. Lawrence
Gulf seemed to rim in the splendour like a huge
bowl of pearl and sapphire brimmed with wind
and fire.

2 Tinkles of sleigh bells and distant laughter, that
seemed like the mirth of wood elves, came from
every quarter.

3 It was pleasantly warm and dimly lighted by the
embers of a fire in the grate.

FEBRUARY

4 For Anne the days slipped by like golden beads on the necklace of the year.

5 It had snowed softly and thickly all through the hours of darkness …

6 … and the beautiful whiteness, glittering in the frosty sunshine, looked like a mantle of charity cast over all the mistakes and humiliations of the past.

7 Charles Dickens, British author of *David Copperfield*, *A Christmas Carol*, and many other classics, was born on this date in 1812. His phrase "prunes, and prism" is a frequent description in the Anne books.

8 … little flurries of snow hissed against the windows ….

9 "Kindred spirits are not so scarce as I used to think. It's
splendid to find out there are so many of them in the world."
Elizabeth von Arnim wrote of "kindred spirits" in one of
L. M. Montgomery's favourite books, *Elizabeth and her
German Garden*, published in 1898. Von Arnim died on this
date in 1941.

10 "It's still February and 'on the convent roof the
snows are sparkling to the moon'…"
  — from Tennyson's "St. Agnes' Eve"

11 "But I'm beginning to think, 'Only a few more
weeks till spring …' "

12 "One stormy evening when the wind was
howling along Spook's Lane, we couldn't go
for a walk, so we came up to my room and drew
a map of fairyland."

13 When they went back to Four Winds the little
house was almost drifted over …

---

14   **St. Valentine's Day**
    Yes, this was romance, the very, the real
thing, with all the charm of rhyme and story
and dream.

---

15   … the third storm of a winter that was to
prove phenomenally stormy had whirled up the
harbour and heaped huge snow mountains about
everything it encountered.

---

16   The hills beyond glistened with the chill,
splendid lustre of moonlight on snow.

17

Every little fir-tree in the long valley sang its own
wild song to the harp of wind and frost.

18

They were having a glorious time and their gay
voices and gayer laughter echoed up and down
the valley, dying away in elfin cadences among
the trees.

19

… the lights of Ingleside gleamed through the
maple grove with the genial lure and invitation
which seems always to glow in the beacons
of a home where we know there is love and
good-cheer and a welcome for all kin, whether of
flesh or spirit.

20 Far on the western hill gleamed a paler but more alluring star.

21 A sled with three shrieking occupants sped past Mr. Meredith to the pond.

22 James Russell Lowell was born on this date in 1819. When Matthew drove to the "Bright River" station to meet the "boy" he and Marilla were planning to adopt, "The little birds sang as if it were/The one day of summer in all the year" —from Lowell's *The Vision of Sir Launfal.*

23 The moonlit air sparkled with frost. The snow
    crisped under her feet.

24 Below her lay the Glen with the white
    harbour beyond.

25 Her walk in the frosty air had stung her cheeks
    into a glowing scarlet.

26 She found her own fireside the pleasantest place in the world....

27 Henry Wadsworth Longfellow, American poet, was born in 1807. Anne reminds Diana — when they are cleaning a closet in preparation for a visit from the famous author Mrs. Charlotte Morgan — that "the gods see everywhere," from Longfellow's "The Builders."

28 ... late winter was listening for the word of spring....

29 Tonight the harbour, lying dark under a crimson sunset, seemed full of implications of "fairylands forlorn" and mysterious isles in uncharted seas.

MARCH

March came in that winter like the
meekest of lambs, bringing days that were
crisp and golden and tingling, each
followed by a frosty pink twilight which
gradually lost itself in an elfland
of moonshine.

1 "I really think the woods are just as lovely in winter as in summer. They're so white and still, as if they were asleep and dreaming pretty dreams."

2 … on a dark, windy March evening … even the clouds scudding over the sky seemed in a hurry….

3 "It's pouring cats and dogs … and listen to the wind."

4 The wind wailed very eerily in the spruces by the window.

MARCH

5 They captured in their ramble all the mysteries
and magics of a March evening.

6 Very still and mild it was, wrapped in great,
white, brooding silence—a silence which was
yet threaded through with many little silvery
sounds which you could hear if you hearkened
as much with your soul as your ears.

7 The girls wandered down a long pineland aisle
that seemed to lead right out into the heart of a
deep-red overflowing winter sunset.

8 Oliver Wendell Holmes was born on this date
in 1841. Holmes' phrase "big heart never liked
little cream pot" is used to describe Captain Jim's
generosity in *Anne's House of Dreams*.

9 … a rosy light was staining the green tips
of the pines.

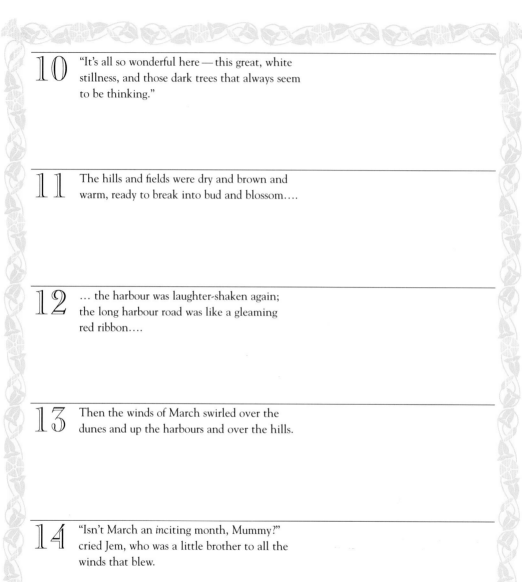

10   "It's all so wonderful here — this great, white stillness, and those dark trees that always seem to be thinking."

11   The hills and fields were dry and brown and warm, ready to break into bud and blossom....

12   ... the harbour was laughter-shaken again; the long harbour road was like a gleaming red ribbon....

13   Then the winds of March swirled over the dunes and up the harbours and over the hills.

14   "Isn't March an *inciting* month, Mummy?" cried Jem, who was a little brother to all the winds that blew.

15   Anne's birthday was in mid-March — perhaps today! "When I woke this morning it seemed to me that everything must be different."

16   The moon was filling the hollows among the white, snowy dunes with magic.

17 **St. Patrick's Day**
   "Just as we entered the gate of Windy Poplars
I noticed a little clump of clover right by the
path. There, right before my eyes were *three*
four-leafed clovers!"

18 The great trees that were so mysterious at
night held out their arms about Ingleside.

19 It had been a busy night for Silversmith Frost and the woods were fairyland.

20 A far-off hill was touched with a crimson spear.

21 **Traditional First Day of Spring**
    Spring was trying out her paces that day … like an adorable baby just learning to walk.

22 Caroline Elizabeth Sarah Norton, author of "Bingen on the Rhine," was born in 1808. At Anne's first concert, Gilbert Blythe recited it, trying to catch her eye when he said the line, "there's another, *not* a sister."

23 Overhead was a hard dark wintry sky; there was what Susan called "a feel" of snow in the air, and a skim of ice over the puddles.

24 A light rain had been falling all day — a little, delicate, beautiful spring rain, that somehow seemed to hint and whisper of mayflowers and wakening violets.

25 The harbour and the gulf and the low-lying shore fields had been dim with pearl-grey mists.

26 A. E. Housman, author of "A Shropshire Lad," was born on this date in 1859. Anne and Diana encountered "brooks not yet 'too broad for leaping' " as they rambled across the Avonlea countryside one fine spring day.

27 But now in the evening the rain had ceased and the mists had blown out to sea.

28 Clouds sprinkled the sky over the harbour like little fiery roses.

29 … the hills were dark against a spendthrift splendour of daffodil and crimson.

30 A great silvery evening star was watching over the bar.

31 A brisk, dancing, new-sprung wind was blowing up from Rainbow Valley, resinous with the odours of fir and damp mosses.

APRIL

Spring had come once more to Green
Gables — the beautiful, capricious,
reluctant Canadian spring, lingering
along through April and May in a
succession of sweet, fresh, chilly days,
with pink sunsets and miracles of
resurrection and growth.

APRIL

1 The maples in Lovers' Lane were red-budded
and little curly ferns pushed up around the
Dryad's Bubble.

2 ... winter was over and gone with the thrill
of delight that spring never fails to bring to
the oldest and saddest as well as to the youngest
and merriest.

3 The spring was abroad in the land....

4 ... almost before Anne realized it, spring had
come again to Green Gables and all the world
was abloom once more.

APRIL

5 "… It must be delightful to come into the world with the Mayflowers and violets."

6 … tiny ferns were unrolling like curly-headed green pixy folk wakening up from a nap.

7 William Wordsworth, born on this date in 1770, is quoted extensively in the Anne books; in *Anne of Avonlea*, Marilla realizes Anne has the gift of "the vision and the faculty divine" (from "The Excursion") and sees everything "apparelled in celestial light" (from "Ode on Intimations of Immortality").

8 Minstrel robins were whistling in the firs and the frogs were singing in the marshes.

9

All the basins among the hills were brimmed
with topaz and emerald light.

10

Lew Wallace, author of *Ben Hur*, was born in
1827. Anne was caught reading a copy of the
popular novel in school when she should have
been studying Canadian history.

11

… they rambled through the park on one of
April's darling days of breeze and blue, when the
harbour was creaming and shimmering beneath
the pearl-hued mists floating over it.

12

The fresh chill air was faintly charged with the
aroma of pine balsam, and the sky above was
crystal clear and blue — a great inverted cup of
blessing.

13 "Spring is singing in my blood today, and the lure of April is abroad on the air."

14 "Everything is new in the spring.... Springs themselves are always so new, too. No spring is ever just like any other spring. It always has something of its own to be its own peculiar sweetness."

15 "See how green the grass is around that little pond, and how the willow buds are bursting."

16 "I want to hunt ferns in the Haunted Wood and
gather violets in Violet Vale."

17 They lingered in the park until sunset, living in
the amazing miracle and glory and wonder of the
springtide....

18 The April wind was filling the pine trees with
its roundelay, and the grove was alive with
robins — great, plump, saucy fellows, strutting
along the paths.

19 "I feel like one of the morning stars that sang for joy," said Anne.

20 "Today has been a day dropped out of June into April."

21 "The snow is all gone and the fawn meadows and golden hills just sing of spring."

22 "I know I heard Pan piping in the little green hollow in my maple bush and my Storm King was bannered with the airiest of purple hazes."

23 William Shakespeare was born on this date in
1564. In *Anne of Green Gables*, Anne muses on
his line from *Romeo and Juliet*: "... a rose/By any
other name would smell as sweet," wondering if
"a rose *would* be as nice if it was called a thistle
or a skunk cabbage."

24 "We've had a great deal of rain lately and I've
loved sitting in my tower in the still, wet hours
of the spring twilights."

25 "But tonight is a gusty, hurrying night ... even
the clouds racing over the sky are in a hurry and
the moonlight that gushes out between them is
in a hurry to flood the world."

26 The land was tender with brand-new, golden-
green, baby leaves.

27 There was an emerald mist on the woods beyond
the Glen. The seaward valleys were full of fairy
mists at dawn.

28 There were pale spring stars shining over fields of
mist, there were pussywillows in the marsh.

29 The first robin was an event; the Hollow was
once more a place full of wild free delight....

30 Anne ... put on spring gladness as a garment and
literally lived in her garden....

MAY

… out in Avonlea the Mayflowers were peeping pinkly out on the sere barrens where snow-wreaths lingered; and the "mist of green" was on the woods and in the valleys.

MAY

1 Away up in the barrens ... the Mayflowers
blossomed out, pink and white stars of sweetness
under their brown leaves.

2 "I'm so sorry for people who live in lands where
there are no Mayflowers," said Anne.

3 "Do you know what I think Mayflowers are,
Marilla? I think they must be the souls of
the flowers that died last summer and this is
their heaven."

4 After the Mayflowers came the violets, and
Violet Vale was empurpled with them.

5   Anne … looked dreamily out of the window,
where big fat red buds were bursting out on the
creeper in response to the lure of the spring
sunshine.

6   Anne sighed and, dragging her eyes from the
witcheries of the spring world, the beckoning
day of breeze and blue, and the green things
upspringing in the garden, buried herself
resolutely in her book.

7   Robert Browning was born on this date in 1812.
Lines from his poem "Evelyn Hope" hint at
Anne's personality in *Anne of Green Gables*:
    "The good stars met in your horoscope,
     Made you of spirit and fire and dew."

8   "… the violets are coming out all purple
down in the hollow below Green Gables and
… little ferns are poking their heads up in
Lovers' Lane …"

9   "Look at that arch of pale green sky over those houses and picture to yourselves what it must look like over the purply-dark beechwoods back of Avonlea."

10   Early oats greened over the red fields; apple orchards flung great blossoming arms about the farmhouses …

11   … and the Snow Queen adorned itself as a bride for her husband.

12   Anne liked to sleep with her window open and let the cherry fragrance blow over her face all night.

13 "Thanksgiving should be celebrated in the spring ... in May one simply can't help being thankful...."

14 "It seems to me, Marilla, that a pearl of a day like this, when the blossoms are out and the winds don't know where to blow from next for sheer crazy delight must be pretty near as good as heaven."

15 "Marilla, look at that apple tree.... It is reaching out long arms to pick its own pink skirts daintily up and provoke us to admiration."

16 "Do you know, I found a cluster of white violets
under that old twisted tree over there today?
I felt as if I had discovered a gold mine."

17 "I stopped by the barrens and picked these
Mayflowers ..."

18 "Everything is calling 'spring' to me ... the
little laughing brooks, the blue hazes on the
Storm King, the maples in the grove ... the
white cherry trees along Spook's Lane, the
sleek and saucy robins ... the creeper hanging
greenly down...."

19 ... all sorts of flowers ... are budding into leaf
and bloom....

20 The moon was shining down on her little garden and sparkling on the harbour.

21 Alexander Pope was born on this date in 1688. A line from his "An Essay on Criticism" describes Anne's enthusiasm for discovering "new worlds of thought" at Queen's: "Hills peeped o'er hills and Alps on Alps arose."

22 A soft, delightful wind was talking to a white apple tree. It was spring … spring … spring!

23 On every side were fields of buttercups and clover where bees buzzed. Now and then they walked through a milky way of daisies.

24 Queen Victoria was born in 1819. On the Queen's Birthday, Anne and Diana discovered an island in the brook and named it "Victoria Island" in her honour.

25 Ralph Waldo Emerson was born in 1803. Anne quoted Emerson one leisurely afternoon: "Remember what Emerson says …'Oh, what have I to do with time?'"

26 Unsuspected tintings glimmered in the dark demesnes of the woods and glowed in their alluring by-ways.

27 The spring sunshine sifted through the young green leaves. Gay trills of song were everywhere.

28 Robins were sprinkling the evening air with flute-like whistles. A great star came out over the white cherry trees.

29 "The flower angel has been walking over the world to-day, calling to the flowers. I can see his blue wings on that hill by the woods."

30 Below her was a big apple-tree, a great swelling cone of rosy blossom.

31 Anne was sitting on the veranda steps, gazing absently over the wonderful bridal world of spring blossom. Beyond the white orchard was a copse of dark young firs and creamy wild cherries, where the robins were whistling madly; for it was evening and the fire of early stars was burning over the maple grove.

JUNE

"Oh, look, there's one little early wild
rose out! Isn't it lovely? Don't you think
it must be glad to be a rose? Wouldn't it
be nice if roses could talk? I'm sure they
could tell us such lovely things."

JUNE

1 The air was sweet with the breath of many apple orchards and the meadows sloped away in the distance to horizon mists of pearl and purple....

2 "... it would be lovely to sleep in a wild cherry tree all white with bloom in the moonshine, don't you think?"

3 "Oh, there are a lot more cherry trees all in bloom! This Island is the bloomiest place."

4 Overhead was one long canopy of snowy fragrant bloom.

5 Below the boughs the air was full of a purple
twilight and far ahead a glimpse of painted sunset
sky shone like a great rose window at the end of
a cathedral aisle.

6 … in the stainless southwest sky, a great crystal-
white star was shining like a lamp of guidance
and promise.

7 "Listen to the trees talking in their sleep….
What nice dreams they must have!"

8 "Don't you feel as if you just loved the world
on a morning like this?"

9 "I'm so glad it's a sunshiny morning. But I like
rainy mornings real well, too…. But I'm glad it's
not rainy today because it's easier to be cheerful
and bear up under affliction on a sunshiny day."

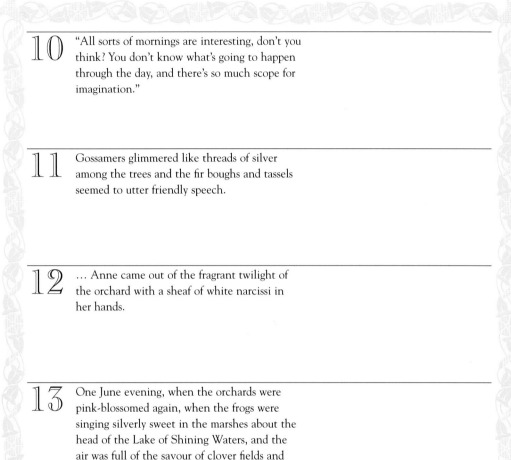

10 "All sorts of mornings are interesting, don't you
    think? You don't know what's going to happen
    through the day, and there's so much scope for
    imagination."

11 Gossamers glimmered like threads of silver
    among the trees and the fir boughs and tassels
    seemed to utter friendly speech.

12 … Anne came out of the fragrant twilight of
    the orchard with a sheaf of white narcissi in
    her hands.

13 One June evening, when the orchards were
    pink-blossomed again, when the frogs were
    singing silverly sweet in the marshes about the
    head of the Lake of Shining Waters, and the
    air was full of the savour of clover fields and
    balsamic fir woods, Anne was sitting by her
    gable window.

14 The apple blossoms were out and the world was
    fresh and young.

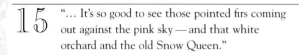

15 "… It's so good to see those pointed firs coming out against the pink sky — and that white orchard and the old Snow Queen."

16 "I'll have a brand new stock of ambition laid in … after three glorious, golden months of vacation."

17 The woods were all gloried through with sunset and the warm splendour of it streamed down through the hill gaps in the west:

18 Outside the Snow Queen was mistily white in the moonshine; the frogs were singing in the marsh beyond Orchard Slope.

19 Charles Haddon Spurgeon was born on this date in 1834. Anne quoted from one of his "John Ploughman" sermons when she returned home after three weeks at Echo Lodge: "… I'm glad to see you dear folks again. 'East, west, home's best.'"

20 … the beautiful world of blossom and love and friendship had lost none of its power to please her fancy and thrill her heart, that life still called to her with many insistent voices.

21 **Traditional First Day of Summer**
    "… I think the summer is going to be lovely."

22 … white moths flew about in the garden and the odour of mint filled the dewy air.

23 The west was a glory of soft mingled hues,
and the pond reflected them all in still softer
shadings.

24 The wind purred softly in the cherry boughs, and
the mint breaths came up to her.

25 "Have the best time you can in the out-of-door
world and lay in a good stock of health and
vitality and ambition to carry you through
next year."

26 "… I'm going to let my imagination run riot for
the summer."

JUNE

27 The robins were singing vespers in the high treetops, filling the golden air with their jubilant voices.

28 White mists were hovering in the silent hollows and violet stars were shining bluely on the brooklands.

29 "I wonder what it would be like to live in a world where it was always June …"

30 Anne felt at peace with the world and herself as she walked down the hill with her basket of flowers in her hand.

JULY

Anne was sitting at her open window
... as she drank in the beauty of the
summer dusk, sweet-scented with
flower-breaths from the garden below and
sibilant and rustling from the stir of the
poplars.

JULY

1 **Canada Day**
"Well, when you can combine patriotism and fun, isn't it all right?"

2 "There was a long row of white birches hanging over the lake and the sunshine fell down through them, 'way, 'way down, deep into the water."

3 … they sat on the big red stones by the Dryad's Bubble and made rainbows in the water with little twigs dipped in fir balsam.

4 **Independence Day (U.S.A.)**
"Oh, look, Diana, what a lovely rainbow! Do you suppose the dryad will come out after we go away and take it for a scarf?"

5 L. M. Montgomery was married to the Rev. Ewan MacDonald on this date in 1911.

6   "Oh, how good it is to be back! Green Gables is
the dearest, loveliest spot in the world."

7   The eastern sky above the firs was flushed faintly
pink from the reflection of the west, and Anne
was wondering dreamily if the spirit of colour
looked like that....

8   ... Anne ... knelt sweetly by her open window
in a great sheen of moonshine and murmured
a prayer of gratitude and aspiration that came
straight from her heart.

9   ... the morning dawned pearly and lustrous in a
sky full of silver sheen and radiance....

10   ... the garden ... was full of airy shadows and
wavering golden lights.

11 "Marilla, look at that big star over Mr. Harrison's maple grove, with all that holy hush of silvery sky about it."

12 Anne was kneeling at the west gable window watching the sunset sky that was like a great flower with petals of crocus and a heart of fiery yellow.

13 The two girls were loitering one evening in a fairy hollow of the brook. Ferns nodded in it, and little grasses were green, and wild pears hung finely-scented, white curtains around it.

14 It was a darkly-purple bloomy night. The air was heavy with blossom fragrance — almost too heavy.

15 One of the fierce summer storms which sometimes sweep over the gulf was ravaging the sea.

JULY

16 The rain was beating down over the shivering fields. The Haunted Wood was full of the groans of mighty trees wrung in the tempest, and the air throbbed with the thunderous crash of billows on the distant shore.

17 Anne saw a fairy fringe of light on the skirts of darkness. Soon the eastern hilltops had a fire-shot ruby rim.

18 William Thackeray was born in 1811. In one of Anne's first letters to Gilbert from Windy Poplars, Anne compares her difficult student Jen Pringle to "Becky Sharp" from Thackeray's *Vanity Fair*.

19 The clouds rolled themselves away into great, soft, white masses on the horizon; the sky gleamed blue and silvery. A hush fell over the world.

20 The morning was a cup filled with mist and glamour.

JULY

---

21 In the corner near her was a rich surprise of
new-blown, crystal-dewed roses.

---

22 The trills and trickles of song from the birds in
the big tree above her seemed in perfect accord
with her mood.

---

23 … the moonlight was raining "airy silver"
through the cherry boughs and filling the east
gable with a soft, dream-like radiance….

24 … they sat one evening in a ferny corner of a clover field and watched the glories of a sunset sky.

25 The road to Lowbridge was a double ribbon of dancing buttercups, with here and there the ferny green rim of an inviting grove.

26 The sky over the birches in the Hollow was showing a faint, silvery-pink radiance.

27 Thomas Campbell, author of "The Battle of Hohenlinden" and "The Downfall of Poland" (two of the poems Anne had memorized from the *Third Royal Reader*), was born on this date in 1777.

28 Tiger lilies were "burning bright" along the walk and whiffs of honeysuckle went and came on the wings of the dreaming wind.

29 "Look at that wave of poppies breaking against the garden wall, Miss Cornelia."

30 Samuel Rogers was born in 1763. Anne encouraged Katherine Brooke to recite Rogers' poem "Genevra" at an Avonlea concert during their Christmas holiday.

31 There was a tang of mint in the air and some unseen roses were unbearably sweet.

AUGUST

Excitement hung around Anne like a
garment, shone in her eyes, kindled in
every feature. She had come dancing up
the lane, like a wind-blown sprite,
through the mellow sunshine and lazy
shadows of the August evening.

AUGUST

1 Birds sang around Green Gables; the Madonna lilies in the garden sent out whiffs of perfume that entered in on viewless winds at every door and window, and wandered through halls and rooms like spirits of benediction.

2 The birches in the hollow waved joyful hands as if watching for Anne's usual morning greeting from the east gable.

3 Rupert Brooke was born in 1887. Lines from his poem "The Song of the Pilgrims" were an epigraph to *Anne's House of Dreams*:
"Our kin
    Have built them temples, and therein
    Pray to the gods we know; and dwell
    In little houses lovable."

4 "Oh, Marilla, there is something in me today that makes me just love everybody I see ..."

AUGUST

5 ... she came home through the twilight, under a great, high-sprung sky gloried over with trails of saffron and rosy cloud....

6 Alfred, Lord Tennyson, was born in 1809. Quotations from many of his works are found throughout the Anne books. A scene from his epic poem *Idylls of the King* inspired Anne to portray the Lady Elaine floating down the river to Camelot.

7 A cool wind was blowing down over the long harvest fields from the rims of firry western hills and whistling through the poplars.

8 One clear star hung above the orchard and the fireflies were flitting over in Lovers' Lane, in and out among the ferns and rustling boughs.

9 Anne ... somehow felt that wind and stars and fireflies were all tangled up together into something unutterably sweet and enchanting.

10

… Anne had the golden summer of her life as far as freedom and frolic went.

11

She walked, rowed, berried and dreamed to her heart's content …

AUGUST

12 Anne breathed deeply, and looked into the clear
sky beyond the dark boughs of the firs.

13 Oh, it was good to be out again in the purity and
silence of the night!

14 How great and still and wonderful everything
was, with the murmur of the sea sounding
through it and the darkling cliffs beyond like
grim giants guarding enchanted coasts.

15 Sir Walter Scott was born on this date in 1771.
Anne was twelve years old when she memorized
the battle canto from Scott's *Marmion*. She
thrilled to its "rushing lines" as she led the cows
home through Lovers' Lane.

16 "Look at that sea, girls — all silver and shadow
and vision of things not seen."

17 … an August afternoon, with blue hazes scarfing
the harvest slopes, little winds whispering elfishly
in the poplars, and a dancing splendour of red
poppies outflaming against the dark coppice of
young firs in a corner of the cherry orchard….

18 … the drive home, through lanes where the
raindrops sparkled on the boughs and little leafy
valleys where the drenched ferns gave out spicy
odours, was delightful.

19 Gilbert stretched himself out on the ferns beside
the Bubble and looked approvingly at Anne.

20 Anne … blithely greeted the fresh day, when the
banners of the sunrise were shaken triumphantly
across the pearly skies.

21 Green Gables lay in a pool of sunshine, flecked with the dancing shadows of poplar and willow.

22 The world was so beautiful that Anne spent ten blissful minutes hanging idly over the garden gate drinking the loveliness in.

23 … the garden was alive with dancing shadows and flickering lights.

AUGUST

24 The garden was a pool of late golden sunshine,
with butterflies hovering and bees booming....

25 Through the open window, by which Anne sat,
blew the sweet, scented, sun-warm air of the
August afternoon....

26 It had been a warm, smoky summer afternoon.

27 The world was a splendour of out-flowering.
The idle valleys were full of hazes.

AUGUST

28
The woodways were pranked with shadows and the fields with the purple of the asters.

29
The moon rose in the silvery sky, empearling the clouds around her. Below, the pond shimmered in its hazy radiance.

30
The wind had fallen asleep in the pinelands and lurid sheets of heat-lightning flickered across the northern skies.

31
Anne went back to Green Gables by way of the Birch Path, shadowy, rustling, fern-scented, through Violet Vale and past Willowmere, where dark and light kissed each other under the firs, and down through Lover's Lane....

SEPTEMBER

It was a September evening and all the
gaps and clearings in the woods were
brimmed up with ruby sunset light. Here
and there the lane was splashed with it,
but for the most part it was already quite
shadowy beneath the maples, and the
spaces under the firs were filled with a
clear violet dusk like airy wine.

1   Lydia Huntley Sigourney, author of "The Dog at His Master's Grave," was born on this date in 1791. Anne offered to recite this "sad and melancholy" poem on her first day of Sunday School in Avonlea.

2   "What a splendid day!" said Anne. "Isn't it good just to be alive on a day like this?"

3   "—maples are such sociable trees," said Anne; "they're always rustling and whispering to you...."

4 ... the light came down sifted through so many
emerald screens that it was as flawless as the
heart of a diamond.

5 ... there was a delightful spiciness in the air and
music of bird calls and the murmur and laugh of
wood winds in the trees overhead.

6 With her chin propped on her hands and her
eyes fixed on the blue glimpse of the Lake of
Shining Waters that the west window afforded,
she was far away in a gorgeous dreamland,
hearing and seeing nothing save her own
wonderful visions.

7 Anne ... was wandering happily in the far end of
the grove, waist deep among the bracken, singing
softly to herself, with a wreath of rice lilies on
her hair as if she were some wild divinity of the
shadowy places....

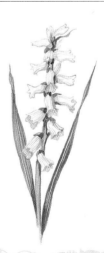

SEPTEMBER

8 She learned her lessons at home, did her chores,
   and played with Diana in the chilly purple
   autumn twilights....

9 The winds were out in their tops, and there is no
   sweeter music on earth than that which the wind
   makes in the fir-trees at evening.

10 "Isn't this evening just like a purple dream,
   Diana? It makes me so glad to be alive. In
   the mornings I always think the mornings
   are best; but when evening comes I think it's
   lovelier still."

11 James Thompson was born on this date in 1700.
   While driving to White Sands, Anne told
   Marilla she knew most of his poem
   "The Seasons" "off by heart."

12 A glance from her window assured her that the
   day would be fine, for the eastern sky behind the
   firs of the Haunted Wood was all silvery
   and cloudless.

13 The air was fresh and crisp, and little smoke-blue
mists curled through the valleys and floated off
from the hills.

14 ... the Avonlea hills came out darkly against the
saffron sky. Behind them the moon was rising out
of the sea that grew all radiant and transfigured
in her light.

15 Anne thought those Friday evening gypsyings over the autumnal hills in the crisp golden air, with the homelights of Avonlea twinkling beyond, were the best and dearest hours in the whole week.

16 A September day on Prince Edward Island hills; a crisp wind blowing up over the sand dunes from the sea …

17 … a long red road, winding through fields and woods, now looping itself about a corner of thick set spruces, now threading a plantation of young maples with great feathery sheets of ferns beneath them….

18 "Oh, this is a day left over from Eden, isn't it, Diana?"

19   "The air has magic in it. Look at the purple in
the cup of that harvest valley, Diana. And oh, do
smell the dying fir!"

20   ... airy fleets of thistledown drifted by on the
wings of a wind that was still summer-sweet with
the incense of ferns in the Haunted Wood.

21   **Traditional First Day of Autumn**
But everything in the landscape around them
spoke of autumn.

22   The sea was roaring hollowly in the distance,
the fields were bare and sere, scarfed with
golden rod ...

23 … the brook valley below Green Gables
overflowed with asters of ethereal purple …

24 … the Lake of Shining Waters was blue —
blue — blue — ; not the changeful blue of
spring, nor the pale azure of summer, but a clear,
steadfast, serene blue, as if the water were past
all moods and tenses of emotion and had settled
down to a tranquility unbroken by fickle dreams.

25 Felicia Dorothea Hemans was born in 1793.
Anne quoted from her poem, "The Woman
on the Field of Battle," just before her final
examinations at Queen's: "I've done my best and
I begin to understand what is meant by the 'joy
of the strife.' "

26 The fine, empurpling dye of sunset still stained
the western skies, but the moon was rising and
the water lay like a great, silver dream in her
light.

27 … the harvest hills were basking in an amber sunset radiance, under a pale, aerial sky of rose and blue.

28 Kate Douglas Wiggin was born on this date in 1856. Anne has often been compared to her popular character, "Rebecca of Sunnybrook Farm."

29 The distant spruce groves were burnished bronze, and their long shadows barred the upland meadows.

30 September slipped by into a gold and crimson graciousness of October.

OCTOBER

October was a beautiful month at Green
Gables, when the birches in the hollow
turned as gold as sunshine and the
maples behind the orchard were royal
crimson and the wild cherry trees along
the land put on the loveliest shades of
dark red and bronzy green, while the
fields sunned themselves in aftermaths.

1   "I'm so glad I live in a world where there are Octobers. It would be terrible if we just skipped from September to November, wouldn't it?"

2   "Look at those maple branches. Don't they give you a thrill — several thrills? I'm going to decorate my room with them."

OCTOBER

3 The orchard, with its great sweeping boughs
that bent to the ground with fruit, proved so
delightful that the little girls spent most of the
afternoon in it, sitting in a grassy corner where
the frost had spared the green ...

4 ... the mellow autumn sunshine lingered
warmly....

5 "I was imagining that I was a frost fairy going
through the woods turning the trees red and
yellow, whichever they wanted to be...."

6 ... she took her way down through the sere
clover field over the log bridge and up through
the spruce grove, lighted by a pale little moon
hanging low over the western woods.

7 Anne sighed and betook herself to the back
yard, over which a young new moon was shining
through the leafless poplar boughs from an
apple-green western sky....

8   ... all the woods were leafless and the fields sere and brown.

9   The sun was just setting with a great deal of purple and golden pomp behind the dark woods west of Avonlea....

10   ... the wind of the autumn night was dancing with the brown leaves.

11   ... they found a road leading into the heart of acres of glimmering beech and maple woods, which were all in a wondrous glow of flame and gold, lying in a great purple stillness and peace.

12   "It's as if the year were kneeling to pray in a vast cathedral full of mellow stained light, isn't it?" said Anne dreamily.

13 "I just want to drink the day's loveliness in ... I feel as if she were holding it out to my lips like a cup of airy wine and I'll take a sip at every step."

14 "How I love the pines! They seem to strike their roots deep into the romance of all the ages."

15 They all sat down in the little pavilion to watch an autumn sunset of deep red fire and pallid gold.

16 To their right lay the harbour, taking on tints of rose and copper as it stretched out into the sunset.

17 "There was such a nice frosty, Octobery smell in the air, blent with the delightful odour of newly plowed fields."

18 "This is one of the days people *feel* alive and every wind of the world is a sister."

19 It was a wonderful day for a drive through a land that was keeping its old lovely ritual of autumn....

20 The calm rims of the upland hills were as blue, the roads as red, the maples as gorgeous, no matter what vehicle you rode in.

21 Samuel Taylor Coleridge was born in 1772. Lines from "Kubla Khan" inspired Anne's son Walter's vision of heaven in *Rainbow Valley*:

"There were gardens bright with sinuous rills
Where blossomed many an incense bearing tree,
And there were forests ancient as the hills
Enfolding sunny spots of greenery."

22 ... moonlit mists were hanging over the harbour and curling like silver ribbons along the seaward glens.

23 It was an evening of grey fog that had crept in from the gulf, swathed the harbour, filled the glens and valleys, and clung heavily to the autumnal meadows.

24 The splendour of colour which had glowed for weeks along the shores of Four Winds Harbour had faded out into the soft grey-blue of late autumnal hills.

25 Thomas Babington Macaulay, author of "Horatius," was born in 1800. Anne's son Jem yearned for his "brave days of old" when men fought "for the ashes of their fathers and the temples of their gods."

26 The little garden, where only marigolds still bloomed, was already hooding itself in shadows.

27 There was the joy of winds blowing in from a darkly blue gulf and the splendour of harvest moons.

28 There were lyric asters in the Hollow and
children laughing in an apple-laden orchard …

29 … clear serene evenings on the high hill pastures
of the Upper Glen and silvery mackerel skies
with dark birds flying across them …

30 … and, as the days shortened, little grey mists
stealing over the dunes and up the harbour.

31 John Keats was born on this date in 1795.
Anne was enchanted by the image of "A magic
casement opening on the foam / Of perilous
seas in fairy lands forlorn" in his "Ode to a
Nightingale."

NOVEMBER

It was nearly dark, for the dull
November twilight had fallen around
Green Gables, and the only light in the
kitchen came from the dancing red
flames in the stove.

NOVEMBER

1   Anne was curled up Turk-fashion on the hearth-rug, gazing into that joyous glow where the sunshine of a hundred summers was being distilled from the maple cordwood.

2   "It's lovely in the woods now. All the little wood things — the ferns and the satin leaves and the crackerberries — have gone to sleep, just as if somebody had tucked them away until spring under a blanket of leaves."

3   William Cullen Bryant was born in 1794. Lines from "A Forest Hymn" came to Anne one evening as she walked the wooded paths of "Kingsport": "'The woods were God's first temples,'" quoted Anne softly. "One can't help feeling reverent and adoring in such a place."

4   Anne ... was ... enjoying the charm of a mild west wind blowing across a newly ploughed field on a grey November twilight and piping a quaint little melody among the twisted firs below the garden....

5   "November is usually such a disagreeable month ... as if the year had suddenly found out that she was growing old and could do nothing but weep and fret over it."

6 "How quiet the woods are today ... not a murmur except that soft wind purring in the treetops!"

7 "How dear the woods are! You beautiful trees! I love every one of you as a friend."

8 "It's beginning to snow, girls ... and there are the loveliest little stars and crosses all over the garden walk."

9   "... shall I go to the park, where there is the lure of grey woods and of grey water lapping on the harbour rocks?"

10   It was November — the month of crimson sunsets, parting birds, deep, sad hymns of the sea, passionate wind-songs in the pines.

11   Anne roamed through the pineland alleys in the park and, as she said, let that great sweeping wind blow the fogs out of her soul.

12 ... the clouds parted and a burst of pale
November sunshine fell athwart the harbour
and the pines ...

13 "Some nights I like the rain — I like to lie in bed
and hear it pattering on the roof and drifting
through the pines."

14 "It feels like snow tonight. I like an evening
when it feels like snow."

15 "The last golden leaf will be blown from the
aspens tonight."

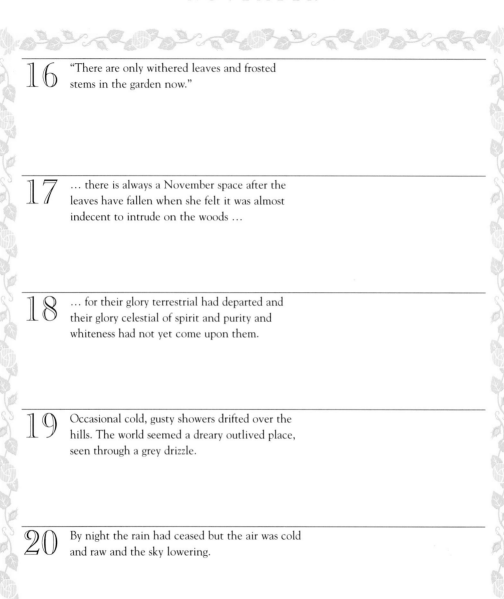

16   "There are only withered leaves and frosted stems in the garden now."

17   … there is always a November space after the leaves have fallen when she felt it was almost indecent to intrude on the woods …

18   … for their glory terrestrial had departed and their glory celestial of spirit and purity and whiteness had not yet come upon them.

19   Occasional cold, gusty showers drifted over the hills. The world seemed a dreary outlived place, seen through a grey drizzle.

20   By night the rain had ceased but the air was cold and raw and the sky lowering.

21 The splendour of colour which had glowed for
weeks along the shores of Four Winds Harbour
had faded out into the soft grey-blue of late
autumnal hills.

22 There came many days when fields and shores
were dim with misty rain, or shivering before the
breath of a melancholy sea-wind....

23 "In November I sometimes feel as if spring could never come again...."

24 The gay little garden of the schoolmaster's bride was rather a forlorn place now, and the Lombardies and birches were under bare poles....

25 But the fir-wood behind the little house was forever green and staunch; and even in November and December there came gracious days of sunshine and purple hazes ...

26 ... the harbour danced and sparkled as blithely as in midsummer, and the gulf was so softly blue and tender that the storm and the wild wind seemed only things of a long-past dream.

27 The moon was rising over the sad, dark sea behind them and transfiguring it.

28 William Blake was born on this date in 1757. The tiger lilies "'burning bright' along the walk" of Anne's *House of Dreams* refer to Blake's "The Tiger": "Tiger, tiger, burning bright."

29 "How the home lights shine out tonight through the dark!" said Anne. "That string of them over the harbour looks like a necklace."

30 L. M. Montgomery was born on this date in 1874, in Clifton, Prince Edward Island.
   This is also the birthday of Canadian Lt. Col. John MacCrae, who wrote "In Flanders Fields," the moving poem of World War I alluded to in *Rilla of Ingleside*.

DECEMBER

… it seemed as if December had
remembered that it was time for winter
and had turned suddenly dull and
brooding, with a windless hush predictive
of coming snow.

DECEMBER

1 The wind had risen and was sighing and wailing
around the eaves and the snow was thudding
softly against the windows, as if a hundred storm
sprites were tapping for entrance.

2 "I'm going home to an old country farmhouse,
once green, rather faded now, set among leafless
apple orchards."

3 "There is a brook below and a December fir wood
beyond, where I've heard harps swept by the
fingers of rain and wind."

4 ... they drove home together under silent,
star-sown depths of sky.

5 ... the white flakes were beginning to flutter
down over the fields and woods, russet and grey
in their dreamless sleep.

DECEMBER

6 Soon the far-away slopes and hills were dim and wraith-like through their gauzy scarfing, as if pale autumn had flung a misty bridal veil over her hair and was waiting for her wintry bridegroom.

7 "It's snowing today, and I'm rapturous."

8 The echoes were at home, over the white river, as silver-clear and multitudinous as ever....

9 It was one of the nights when the storm-wind hurtles over the frozen meadows and black hollows, and moans around the eaves like a lost creature, and drives the snow sharply against the shaking panes.

10 … how lovely it was to wake up in the night and hear the first snowstorm of the winter around your tower and then snuggle down in your blankets and drift into dreamland again.

11   Out in the open country the world was all
golden-white and pale violet, woven here and
there with the dark magic of spruces and the
leafless delicacy of birches.

12   The low sun behind the bare woods seemed
rushing through the trees like a splendid god....

13   The snow crisped under the runners; the music
of the bells tinkled through the ranks of tall
pointed firs, snow-laden.

14   The White Way of Delight had little festoons of
stars tangled in the trees.

15   And on the last hill but one they saw the great
gulf, white and mystical under the moon but not
yet ice-bound.

DECEMBER

16 "I've always found it hard to resist the lure of a moonlight night."

17 John Greenleaf Whittier was born in 1807. On Anne's trip with Marilla to White Sands, the Shore Road is described as "woodsy and wild and lonesome," a phrase from Whittier's "Cobbler Keezar's Vision."

18 They went through Lover's Lane, full of lovely tree shadows, and across fields where little fir trees fringed the fences … and through open glades that were like pools of silver.

19 How beautiful Green Gables was on a winter night!

20 Enchantment had been at work the night before. A light snow had fallen and the powdered firs were dreaming of a spring to come and a joy to be.

21 **Traditional First Day of Winter**
Silence was everywhere, save for the staccato clip of a horse trotting over the bridge.

22 The plum pudding was concocted and the Christmas tree brought home.

23 They wandered about, gathering creeping spruce and ground pine for wreaths … even some ferns that kept green in a certain deep hollow of the woods all winter ..

24 **Christmas Eve**
The world was lost in a white passion of snowstorm. The window-panes were grey with drifted snow. The Scotch pine was an enormous sheeted ghost.

25 **Christmas Day**
Christmas morning broke on a beautiful white
world ... just enough snow fell softly in the night
to transfigure Avonlea.

26 "Oh, hasn't it been a brilliant evening?" sighed
Anne ...

27 They went for long walks ... through Lover's
Lane and the Haunted Wood, where the very
silence seemed friendly ...

DECEMBER

28 But what an evening it was! What silvery satin roads with a pale green sky in the west after a light snowfall!

29 Orion was treading his stately march across the heavens, and hills and fields and woods lay around them in a pearly silence.

30 Rudyard Kipling was born on this date in 1865. Anne's cat Rusty was compared to Kipling's "The Cat That Walked by Himself" in *Anne of the Island*.

31 **New Year's Eve**
The old year did not slip away in a green twilight, with a pinky-yellow sunset. Instead, it went out with a wild, white bluster and blow.

"After all," Anne had said to Marilla once,
"I believe the nicest and sweetest days are not those
on which anything very splendid or wonderful or
exciting happens, but those that bring simple little
pleasures, following one another softly, like pearls
slipping off a string."

DESIGN, ART DIRECTION AND TYPOGRAPHY

Pronk&Associates

ILLUSTRATION

Bernadette Lau: Jan. 22, Feb. 19, 22, March 17, July 10, Aug. 11, Sept. 13, Oct. 2, Nov. 6, 21, Dec. 6, 10, 25

Carol Paton: Jan. 25, Feb. 14, April 1, 8, 12, 16, 22, May 4, 8, 12, 19, 23, 27, June 4, 18, 22, 26, July 6, 27, Aug. 4, 20 27, Sept. 7, 18, 22, 26, Oct. 27, Nov. 15, 26, Dec. 24, credit page

Barbara Massey: cover, opposite opening quote, all month-openers and opposite month-openers, all end-of-month flowers, Jan. 11, Feb. 3, March 4, 27, April 13, June 5, Aug. 21, Oct. 13

Margo Stahl: opening quote, Jan. 8, Feb. 18, March 15, April 23, May 13, June 8, July 21, Sept. 1, Oct. 16, Nov. 9 closing quote, opposite closing quote